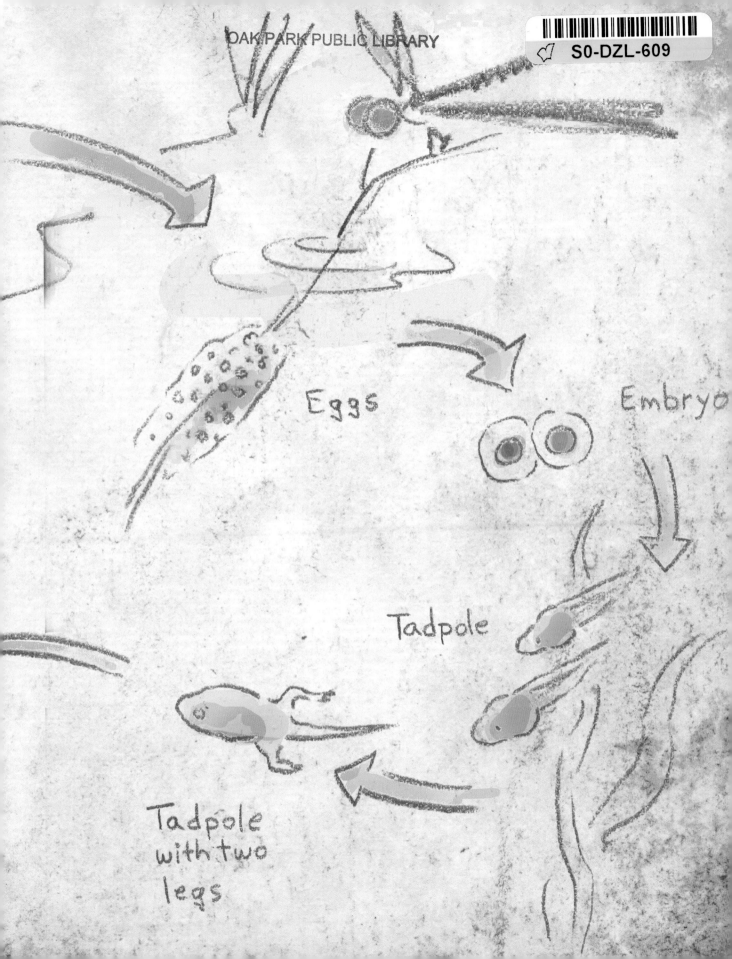

Eggs

Embryo

Tadpole

Tadpole
with two
legs

Lilliana and the Frogs

Harbour Publishing Co. Ltd.

P.O. Box 219, Madeira Park, BC, V0N 2H0

www.harbourpublishing.com

Edited by Sarah Harvey

Printed and bound in South Korea

Harbour Publishing acknowledges the support of the Canada Council for the Arts, the Government of Canada, and the Province of British Columbia through the BC Arts Council.

Library and Archives Canada Cataloguing in Publication

Title: Lilliana and the frogs / Scot Ritchie.

Names: Ritchie, Scot, author, illustrator.

Identifiers: Canadiana (print) 20200246437 | Canadiana (ebook) 20200246445 | ISBN 9781550179347 (hardcover) | ISBN 9781550179354 (EPUB)

Classification: LCC PS8635.I825 L55 2020 | DDC jC813/.6—dc23

LILLIANA

AND THE

FROGS

by *Scot Ritchie*

HARBOUR

Chorus frogs are very small.

Just like Lilliana.

Chorus frogs sing at night.
Lilliana loves to listen.